CAMP ADVENTURE

Elizabeth Elbert

TO SOW IS TO HARVEST

Scythe Publications, Inc.

A Division of Winston-Derek Publishers Group, Inc.

First printing

PUBLISHED BY SCYTHE PUBLICATIONS, INC.
Nashville, Tennessee 37205

Library of Congress Catalog Card No: 92-59948
ISBN: 1-55523-576-X

Printed in the United States of America

To Janice, Joy, Megan, Beth and Robert,
my companions in adventure.

ONE

Hi! I'm Libby Compton. Well, actually my name is Elizabeth Ann Compton, and I'm twelve years old. Next year I'm going into seventh grade at Johnson School in Arborville, Michigan. I'm excited about that. I have four really close friends, and we do everything together. That's why we all decided if one of us went to summer camp, we all had to go.

And our folks said, O.K. Maybe they were even glad to have someone else take care of us for awhile. Anyway, yesterday I was all packed up for Camp Adventure. I felt a little funny when I hugged my mom goodbye. This is the first time I've left her since my dad died two years ago. I noticed her eyes looked kind of shiny, but she told me to have a good time and to phone if I needed anything. I felt a little sniffley too, so I hid my face in my little brother's hair and hugged him hard. Charles is three and he is a little demon. Then Mr. Davis and his daughter Rachel came to pick me up in their station wagon. Joy and Janie Field, my friends who are twins, were already in the car.

Mr. Davis got out and took my sleeping bag, and pillow, and suitcase and piled them in the back. I got in beside Janie and Joy, and we all grinned at each other.

"This is great," I said.

Janie nodded. "I just hope we get a nice counselor, that's all."

The twins look alike. They have light-brown hair and blue eyes. Their hair is long, actually below their shoulders, and they love to wear head-bands. The teachers in school can't tell them apart, but I can. I'm the tallest of all of us. My hair is dark brown, and I wear it in a ponytail.

Joy grinned. "Well, the important thing is that we're all in the same cabin. Right, Rachel?"

Rachel turned and looked at us as her dad started the car. "That's right. I told my folks I really didn't want to go if I had to room with girls I don't know." Rachel has beautiful dark skin and a cute short Afro haircut. She's been my friend since nursery school. I knew her even before the twins.

"Nothing to worry about," I said. "We're together."

"O.K.," Mr. Davis said, "now for Tracy Green." He drove down the street and pulled up beside a big brick apartment building. I could see Tracy at the second-floor window, watching for us. It's easy to spot Tracy, even at a distance. She has the reddest hair you've ever seen, and green eyes and freckles. Tracy is the shortest of all of us, and the plumpest. Every time she eats a candy bar she says, "I shouldn't be eating this," and she laughs. Tracy does a lot of laughing, even though her parents are divorced. Her mom lives here in Arborville, and her dad lives in Chicago. Tracy was supposed to spend the whole summer in Chicago with him, but he said it was O.K. for her to go to camp for three weeks first. We were all happy about that.

I opened the door and Tracy climbed past me into the back seat, dragging her sleeping bag and duffel over my feet.

"Hi gang," she shouted. "Are they supposed to give us lunch at that camp? I'm starved already."

"It's only 10:30," Joy said.

And Janie said at the same time, "Didn't you have any breakfast?"

2

"Sure," Tracy grinned, "hours ago."

"Like 7:30?" Rachel smiled.

"Right," Tracy answered. "That's what I said: hours ago!"

Mr. Davis started the car. "The schedule mentioned lunch, Tracy. I'm sure they won't let you starve."

As we drove out of Arborville we were all too excited to sit still. We kept looking at each other and giggling. The drive was only thirty-five minutes, but it seemed much longer. I was thinking of the contents of my suitcase: 6 blouses, 6 underpants, 3 jeans, 3 skirts, 2 swimming suits, 4 shorts, 10 socks, 2 pairs of shoes, 2 p.j.s, a bathrobe, a sweater, and all those little things like soap, toothpaste, and dental floss. I suddenly remembered something that I had left on the bureau at home.

"Flashlight," I said out loud. Eight eyes looked at me in surprise. "I forgot my flashlight. Don't you remember? We were supposed to bring a mirror, a compass, and a *flashlight*. Mine's at home."

Rachel said, "You can share mine with me."

"But suppose I have to go to the bathhouse at night."

Rachel shrugged. "You can reach under my pillow and get it, or you can wake me up to go with you. Don't worry about it!"

We knew when we reached the camp. There was a big wooden arch over the road. Burned into it in big letters was the name, CAMP ADVENTURE. We all cheered. Mr. Davis drove up a sandy road to a cottage that was labeled OFFICE. We all climbed out of the car and crowded into the room behind him. A tall blonde woman in a brown uniform shook hands with him as he introduced himself.

She said, "I'm Irene Scott, director of Camp Adventure." She smiled at us. "Everyone calls me Scotty." She looked at some papers on her desk. "Let's see, you are all in the

3

Alpine Cabin, right? That's down the hill in our twelve and thirteen-year-old section. We call that area our Mountain Girls."

Mr. Davis smiled. "What ages come to Camp Adventure?"

"Our youngest girls are eight," Scotty said. "They are in the Sea Girls section with nine and ten-year-olds. Our oldest group is the Desert Girls. They are fourteen and fifteen. All of the groups come together for meals and some campfires, and swimming. But Crafts and Interest Groups will be just with the other Mountain Girls."

Joy and Janie were wiggling with excitement. "Can we see our cabin now?" Janie asked.

Scotty nodded. "Yes. Drive down the mountain pass to the left, Mr. Davis. Your counselor is Theresa, girls. We all call her Terry. Her helpers are Robin and Lucy."

Joy asked, "Does a counselor sleep in the cabin with us?" I could tell from her voice she hoped not.

"Oh no," Scotty said, "just you five girls. The counselors have their own cabin right in the middle of the Mountain Section. There are nine cabins of Mountain Girls."

"Forty-five Mountain Girls," Tracy said. She was quick at math.

Scotty smiled, "That's right. Forty-five girls in each section. One-hundred-thirty-five, all together." We heard another car drive up and some girls got out laughing.

"Please drive them down now, Mr. Davis," Scotty said. "See you later, girls."

We pushed our way out of the room as the next group came in. We really felt excited. It even smelled like a camp: a mixture of dust and evergreens and lake water. But I was awfully glad to be with my friends. I would have been kind of nervous if I was coming alone. We drove down to our area

4

and found our cabin just as a dark-haired girl came up. She had a uniform just like Scotty's.

"I'm Terry, your counselor," she said. She had a nice smile. "That's my cabin three doors down. Give me two days and I'll have all your names straight." She put her arms on Joy and Janie's shoulders. "Except maybe for you two! Lunch is at 12:30. They blow the bugle to tell you when to come. The dining hall is the building on the top of the hill. That's the bathhouse over there in the trees. The rule is, 'Lights Out' at nine!" She waved. "Unpack now. I'll see you at lunch."

Tracy had already gone into our cabin. "What did she mean, 'Lights Out?' We don't have a light in here!"

Mr. Davis smiled as he took our stuff out of the car. "That means it's sleep-time—stop talking, and get some shut-eye."

Rachel pulled her bag up the two steps, as I looked at the cabin. Or was it a tent? The bottom half was a cabin with screen windows and a wooden floor, but the top half was a tent. There was a screen door and rolled-up canvas panels that covered the windows when it rained. Tracy was right. There was no light, no heat, in fact no electricity at all.

"We're living close to nature," I said, as I picked up my sleeping bag. "I think that's what they call it." My words sounded rather cross and I was really terribly excited, so I added, "At least we're protected if a bear comes."

"A bear?" Tracy echoed.

"A squirrel more likely," Joy said.

"Or a woodchuck," Janie added. "They're darling."

We were all in the cabin by this time, and looking around. There were five cot-beds, two on each side under the windows, and one across the back. The twins grabbed the two on the right by sitting on them. Tracy took the front one on the left. I looked at Rachel. "Which do you want?"

She shrugged a little. "Which do you?"

"I don't care."

"O.K." she said. "I'll take the one at the end of Tracy's."

That left the one along the back for me. I went and sat on it, looking out the screen window into the huge trees behind us. There was something kind of awesome about being this close to the trees with only screen and canvas around us .

"Well, are you all set?" Mr. Davis asked. He put an arm around Rachel. "I have to go, Honey." Rachel gave him a tight hug and he ruffled her Afro with his hand. For just a moment I remembered what it was like to have a dad pat your hair. There was something really special about it.

We all thanked Mr. Davis for driving us, and then he left. Rachel stood at the door until his car turned up the hill.

"What do we do now?" Tracy said. "How long till we eat?"

I was the only one who had brought a watch, but the twins had a big wind-up clock. We set the clock from my watch, 12:10. The clock made such a loud tick I wondered if it would keep me awake.

"O.K." I said, "Let's get organized. Time to unpack."

"I read in the camp letter that the neatest cabin in each section wins a prize," Joy said.

"That's right," Janie added. "Also we all have chores to do, a different thing each week."

I looked up from shaking out my sleeping bag. "Chores? Mom didn't mention that."

"Oh sure," Janie said. "You know: help with the dishes one day, set the table another, clean the bathhouse another. I can't remember what the other jobs are."

"I know three more," Joy added. "Wiping off the dining-room tables, putting the food on, and collecting wood for the campfire."

6

Tracy sniffed indignantly. "Come to camp and work!" she said. "I thought this was a vacation."

"I guess I did too, although I don't mind," I said.

Rachel sat on her bed. "I think the idea is that we're learning to take responsibility."

"Is that what you call it?" Tracy grinned. "I call it cheap labor."

At that moment I screamed. I didn't mean to, but crawling toward me was the biggest Daddy-Long-Legs I'd ever seen. I'm not really crazy about bugs and spiders at any time, and living with them is something new to me.

"What's the matter," Joy shouted.

I pointed at the Daddy-Long-Legs.

"Is that all?" Joy said. She walked over and picked it up by the leg, carried it to the door, and tossed it out gently.

"You'd better get use to those," Janie said wisely. "There're probably a lot of them living in this tent."

I shuddered.

"Joy loves them," Janie added. "She thinks she might be a zoologist when she grows up, you know."

"Well not me!" I muttered.

There was one table and two chairs at the front of our cabin. We each had two hooks by our bed, for our bathrobe and sweater, I guess. On the back of the door there were five more hooks. We decided those would be good for wet raincoats and umbrellas. Everything else had to be kept in the suitcases or duffel bags under our beds. We had just finished setting up when the bugle blew.

"Lunch," Tracy shouted, and we all ran for the door.

The dining hall was called Hilltop House because it was at the top of a very steep hill. I felt breathless by the time we reached it, but the view was great. The lake was right below us, and we could see the top of our cabin. It was a hard climb up, but we knew it would be fun to run down afterwards.

We sat at a table with girls from two other cabins. The huge room was filled with campers and counselors. Scotty stood up and welcomed everyone. She said she knew everything was new to us right now, but that by tomorrow we would be Old Hands. Terry was sitting at the table with us. Since none of us had been assigned chores yet, she just picked Rachel and me to serve the table today. She said Joy and Janie could clean off afterwards. We went to the kitchen and picked up big bowls of beef stew, applesauce, carrot sticks, brown bread, oatmeal cookies, and milk. At home I don't like stew very much, but here it tasted great. I guess, like Tracy, I was hungrier than I thought. I had a feeling I might be eating things at camp that I never eat at home.

After lunch we went back to our Mountain Area. We all sat down on a grassy slope, and Terry talked to us. She said that every morning, after chores, we would have Crafts, and then Free Time. In the afternoons there was always swimming, and then we do different things different days: boating, hiking, games, nature walks. There were also special Interest Groups: drama, science, music, puppets, even a math and French group. Every night from 7:30 to 8:30 was Campfire time, sometimes with the whole camp and sometimes just the Mountain Girls by themselves. It all sounded great. She said this afternoon we could sign up for the Interest Group we wanted, and there were rowboats and canoes we could use if we knew how to swim already. She said we could look around the camp, also. There was a little one-room library, and a small Infirmary with three beds in it, in case someone felt sick. She introduced us to our assistant counselors, Robin and Lucy. I grinned at the twins a little because Robin was very tall and Lucy was very short, but they both looked friendly. Then we met Beth and Neil. Beth had black curly hair and was very pretty. Terry told us she was the camp nurse. Neil was her husband. They had just been married two weeks, and Neil was the camp handyman, but during the year he was going to college to become a teacher. He was tall and blonde. I thought he was really good-looking. It was hard to look at anyone else while Neil was standing there smiling. Beth told us that they lived in a room behind the Infirmary. She said if we ever felt sick, just come and tell her. She looked so nice, I decided she would be easy to talk to.

After the meeting, I signed up to be part of the drama group. Janie picked the music group, and Joy picked the science group because she wanted to study insects. Ugh! Rachel joined the French group because she wanted to impress her folks, and Tracy chose the math-games group.

"Don't any of you guys like to act?" I said.

Tracy laughed. "Act up, sure! But not in a play."

"Well, everyone to her own taste," I muttered.

"Said the old lady as she kissed the cow," Janie and Joy said right together, and fell on each other laughing.

That evening we had our first campfire. It was gorgeous. The sky turned from pink to dark blue to black, and the fire sent sparks shooting up into the darkness like wiggly worms. We sang, and Scotty told stories. It turned cool, and I was glad I had on my warm sweater.

Afterwards we hurried to get into our sleeping bags. I gave Tracy back her flashlight, and everything was dark. I heard some frogs croaking from the lake. Then the bugle blew Taps from Hilltop. It sounded sweet and kind of sad. As Taps ended I looked out at the dark trees. It was strange; I

9

could still hear the last note of the bugle. Then I realized, it wasn't Taps I was hearing. It was a mosquito buzzing in my ear on the same note. I slapped my cheek so hard, it took me a long time to go to sleep.

There was a list of chores posted on our bath house the next morning. We ran to see what our jobs would be. For the first three days Tracy and I were on bathroom duty. Rachel was on dining hall crew, and Janie and Joy were firewood collectors.

Rachel groaned. "I don't see why they don't put us all on the same job."

Terry was walking past us and heard what she said. She smiled at Rachel. "Don't you want to make some new friends while you're here?"

"Well sure, but—"

"This is the group you will be with for everything. At the end of the three weeks you'll all feel as though they are sisters."

Rachel grinned. "O.K., if you say so."

It seemed to me that Terry was right, at least until Tracy and I reported to the bath house. Lucy was in charge there today. She told us that our duties were to wash out the basins, scrub the toilets and showers, and mop the floor.

"There are eight of you. If you get right to work it should only take about twenty minutes. She handed a sponge and soap powder to Tracy and two other girls, then gave me a string mop and a bucket. She gave another bucket to the girl behind me.

"Here, Ursula," she said, "let's see how quickly you can do this."

I turned and looked at the girl. She had kind of straight messy hair and she looked really cross. It surprised me.

"Fill the buckets from the wall-tap there," Lucy said. "All right. You all know what to do now?" She smiled and went out.

Actually it was sort of fun. I felt like a sailor scrubbing the deck of a ship. I put the mop in the water, squeezed it, and started on the floor. Suddenly I felt a splash against my leg and water started to run into my shoe. I looked at Ursula in surprise. She was slapping her mop against the floor hard, not even bothering to squeeze it out.

"Hey," I said, "you're getting me wet."

She frowned at me.

"This is just stupid . . . I hate it!"

One of the other girls said, "Oh, calm down, Ursula."

Tracy looked up from the basin she was scrubbing. "Don't be such a poor sport," she said matter-of-factly.

Ursula threw her mop across the floor. "I'm not a poor sport," she shouted, "and I'm not going to stay here and be insulted." She marched out the door. The rest of us just looked at each other. Finally a pretty girl with braids spoke.

"I'm in her cabin. I'm Heather."

"I'm Libby," I said. "That's Tracy. What's the matter with Ursula?"

Heather shook her head. "I don't know. She gets mad so quickly, and when I woke up last night, I heard her sniffing. I think she was crying."

One of the other girls said, "Shall I go and get Lucy?"

Heather sighed. "No, why don't we just do it without her. I'll talk to her later."

12

We all worked fast and twenty-five minutes later we were finished. But my shorts were wet, and I was still annoyed. I said so to Tracy as we walked back to the cabin. "I hope we don't have to see too much of her!"

"I hope not," Tracy said, "but Heather is nice."

"The other girls seemed nice too. I think some of them are in the Rockies cabin. I'm glad Ursula isn't next door."

I changed my clothes in the cabin and then went to the Crafts building. On the way I passed Terry talking to Ursula. Terry looked very firm and Ursula was staring at the ground not saying anything. I felt sort of sorry for her.

Peggy, the crafts teacher, told us we had choices as to what we would like to make. She showed us some samples. I decided to work on a copper bracelet for my mom. All five of us were together for crafts. That was fun. Joy was making a bead belt, and Janie a bead necklace. Rachel chose to sew a leather wallet, and Tracy was making a clay pot which she was going to paint and fire later. All these choices looked so good, I started to think about what I would do for my second choice. I love crafts. The two hours went too fast, but at least we would have it every day.

After lunch we had a free hour to rest or read, or just wander around. We went to our cabin and I told the other girls about Ursula.

"She sounds weird!" Rachel said.

Just then Terry rapped on our door. "Mail Call," she said. "Only this didn't come through the mail." She handed a package to Joy and Janie. "Mr. Davis gave me this yesterday. It's from your folks, girls. He said it was a surprise, but he was not to give it to you until you were in the cabin. Then he forgot. I meant to give it to you last night, but I forgot too." She grinned and left.

13

We all crowded around the twins. "I think I know what it is," Janie said.

Joy nodded. "I hope you're right."

We all knew that the twins can read each other's minds. It's amazing!

Tracy licked her lips. "I hope it's something to eat."

Janie and Joy gave a shout of pleasure as they tore the paper off the package. It was a big box of assorted chocolate cookies and cakes.

"Mom remembered," Janie said.

Joy nodded. "We asked her to send us the biggest box of cookies she could find."

"We thought the meals might be awful," Janie added.

They handed the box around to all of us, and we each took three. The Brownies were the best thing I ever tasted.

"Now don't mention this to anyone outside of this cabin," Joy said.

Janie added, "We want them to last as long as possible." She handed the box to Joy. "You put it in your duffel-bag tonight. Tomorrow I get it."

"Fair enough," Joy said, and put the cookies under her bed. We all grinned at our delicious secret.

Interest Groups were scheduled after rest-time. I went alone to Drama, which met in Hilltop. I saw that this group was open to girls of all ages. As I sat on a bench, the drama counselor stood up.

"I'm Claire," she said. "I'm glad we have a big group because we can pick a play with a good cast. Of course, if some of you prefer to work on scenery, or costumes, or props, that's fine too. We can also decide if we want to have music at the beginning and end."

This was starting to sound exciting. I love acting. I hoped I would get a part in the play. It was then that I looked around and saw Ursula on the bench in front of me. Oh, no! Now I had to be with her every day. What bad luck.

Claire went on speaking. "We only have three weeks, and I would like to give the play for the parents the last day of camp. Would you like that?" We all nodded. "Good. Now I thought it might be fun to do *Snow White and The Seven Dwarfs.* You girls can act dwarfs just as well as boys can, and the prince can be acted by one of you tall ones." She looked at a girl sitting on the front row. "Someone like you would make a fine prince." The girl smiled. I thought with her short hair she really would make a good prince.

"The characters—as you probably all know—are the queen-witch, Snow White, the prince, the seven dwarfs, and we'll change the huntsman to a woman, perhaps a big cook or servant to the queen. Since we won't have time for a complicated makeup change, let's have one of you act the queen and another the witch, although really they are one character. That's twelve speaking parts, but we still have other acting parts such as the servants in the castle and the animals in the forest. I'm sure all of you can have parts who want to act."

She shuffled some pages in her hand. "Today let's have some try-outs for the speaking roles. Put up your hands so I can count you, if you want to read. And when you come up tell me which parts you think you would like."

I put my hand up. I saw Ursula's hand go up too. Quite a few of us wanted to read. When my turn came I asked to read for the queen, the witch, and Snow White. I tried to make them sound really different. Claire smiled when I finished. A few minutes later, Ursula came up. She did not look at me, but she asked to read for the same three parts.

When we were all finished, Claire said, "That's good. You all did well, and everyone will be part of it in one way or another. I'll think about it tonight, and tell you the cast tomorrow."

I was so excited, how could I wait twenty-four hours before I knew? The part I really wanted was Snow White, but probably all the girls wanted it. I wondered if Neil and Beth would come and see the play. I would like Neil to see me act Snow White.

I ran down the hill to the cabin. Janie and Joy were already there. Joy was trying to catch a moth with a butterfly net, and Janie was blowing notes on a recorder.

"Wow," I said, "progress is being made. I"m going to be in a play."

Rachel came up as I spoke. "What part do you have?" she asked.

"I don't know yet. I'll find out tomorrow."

Tracy banged open the door. "Come on, you guys. We're supposed to be on the beach in five minutes."

We all pulled out our swimming suits and rushed getting them on. By the time we got to the lake a bunch of girls were standing around, and the teacher, Sue, was talking.

"We have three levels of swimmers," she said, "Red Caps are the beginners." She pointed to a raft a little way out in the water. "Green Caps are the intermediate. They are supposed to be able to swim to that first raft." Quite a bit farther out, was another raft. "Blue Caps are our top group. They swim all the way out there. They can also take junior life-saving classes, if they like. We will give you swimming lessons whichever group you're in. We will also give you boating instruction, when you can swim to the Green Cap raft." She looked at us seriously. "Our most important swimming rule, girls, is that you must never go in unless a counselor is here. We also use the Buddy system. When I blow my whistle you must grab your Buddy's hand and raise it. Do you have any questions?"

One girl raised her hand. "I'm not sure how far I can swim. All my swimming has been in a pool."

Sue smiled. "Don't worry; we'll find out tomorrow. We will test each one of you, and give you the proper colored cap."

Tomorrow! Why did everything have to be tomorrow? I was a little nervous about the swimming. I only did the dog-paddle, and that second raft looked really far out. I knew the twins were good swimmers, but I was not sure about Rachel and Tracy. Wouldn't it be awful if I was the only Red Cap?

"Now you are not going to swim today because I have been talking to you too long," Sue said, "but just for fun, why don't we have a tug-of-war?" She pulled a long rope from under the dock and divided us into two groups. My heart sank when I saw that Rachel and Tracy were on the other side, but fortunately Joy and Janie were with me.

"Pull your hardest," Janie said. "Forget about cabin loyalty."

We pulled. We really did. For a moment it felt as though we were moving the rope to our side. I dug in my heels firmly and leaned back as hard as I could, but then I began to slip.

Joy shouted, "Pull harder!"

But little by little the rope was moving to the other side. We were skidding across the sand, and falling into each other. A big cheer want up as the rope went over the middle line. We saw Rachel and Tracy jumping up and down waving their arms.

"Our own cabin-mates," Janie said. "A fine thing!"

"I'm not sure they deserve any more cookies," Joy laughed.

The campfire that night was in our own Mountain area. Terry told us to break a stick from a bush and peel it. We picked green ones because we had a feeling we might be putting them into the fire.

Tracy's eyes began to shine. "I think I know what we're going to do," she said.

Terry passed around four Graham crackers to each of us, and a bar of chocolate, and two marshmallows.

"S'mores," Tracy said. "I thought so."

We toasted the marshmallows and put them inside the Graham crackers with the chocolate. It tasted simply yummy. We sat on the logs around the fire, licking our fingers and singing rounds, as it turned dark.

"I simply love this place," Tracy said. "This is living!"

We all grinned at each other, thinking of the cookies in the cabin. After all, two S'mores don't fill up a hungry girl!

THREE

The next day when I went to Drama Class I was so excited I felt rather sick to my stomach. I sat on the bench halfway back, waiting for everyone to arrive. When we were all there, Claire stood up.

"You all read so well yesterday it was hard to choose parts, but I think this will be a good cast." She looked at the paper in her hand. "Queen—Jane Morgan; Prince—Joan Dow; Witch—Ursula Wagner; Snow White—Libby Compton; First Dwarf—" She was still speaking, but I did not hear a word after that. I was so excited. I was Snow White! But there was something else. She had said Ursula was the witch. Ursula would be acting with me every day now. In the play, she would be giving me a poison apple because she wanted me dead. I felt kind of funny about it. I looked over at her. She was not looking at me, and she did not seem to be excited, the way I felt. Her face just looked glum.

Claire was saying, "Now the rest of you who want to act can choose between being people in the palace, or animals in the forest." She walked along the row, handing a script to each person who had a speaking part. "I have marked your lines in red. See if you can learn them in the next two days. Today we'll read through the play to get the feel of it. Those of you who have non-speaking parts must pay attention too. You will be acting even if you do not speak. As we read the play today, think of how you can act your part. There are lots of things you can do to show what kind of character you are."

Then Claire asked those of us who had scripts to come up and sit on the front row. She said she would be the narrator, and she began, "Once upon a time . . ." Then the wicked queen began to speak. She was very good. She sounded proud and vain. When I spoke I tried to sound innocent and kind. We read to the part where the queen drinks the magic drink and changes into the old witch. Claire explained that the queen would step behind a curtain with the drink in her hand, and Ursula would come out, old and grinning.

Claire turned to Ursula. "The witch is wicked, remember, but she is clever too. You must sound like that."

Ursula began to speak. Her voice was old and shaky, but she sounded kind of gleeful too. I could not believe she was such a good actress. When we came to her scene with me and the apple, she made her voice silky-smooth. "Just a little bite, Dearie. Just one bite, and your dreams will come true."

In the play Snow White is unsure. The old woman seemed to be nice, but there was something about her eyes that was almost frightening. I was almost frightened too. As we stood up to read our parts, I felt myself backing away from her nervously.

"Good," Claire said, "both of you. That's exactly right."

We read to the end of the play, and everyone clapped. I started to smile at Ursula, but she looked away. Now that she was not acting, her face looked glum again.

"Study your lines tonight," Claire said to all of us. "Tomorrow we will plan the movements. Then the next day, no scripts! Can you do that?"

As I walked down the hill, Janie ran up to me. "Music was great!" she said. "How did Drama go?"

"Just fine. I'm Snow White. Ursula's the witch." Janie made a face. "She's a really good actress," I said. "Wait till you see the play."

"Yeah, but she's not acting. She is a witch!" Janie laughed.

I smiled, but I felt badly about it. Being with someone who would not look at you or speak to you, except when she is acting, is hard. All the other girls were friendly. I had even decided at chores this morning to be nice to Ursula, but she was not in the bath house with us. Heather said she had asked to be moved to the dish-washing group, and Terry had let her go. I wondered if it was to get away from me.

Back at the cabin, we found Joy rubbing some medicine into a swollen place on her arm.

"What happened, Sis?" Janie asked.

Joy made a face. "We were on an insect hike. I was following a butterfly, and didn't notice the bees."

"Bees! Are you sure you want to be in that group?"

Joy shrugged. "Yeah. It was my fault. The bees were just doing what bees do."

"Which is why I stay away from them," Janie said, and hugged Joy.

Rachel and Tracy came in the cabin at the same time.

"Swimming suits, everybody," Tracy shouted.

My heart sank as I pulled out my suitcase. I had been so excited about getting Snow White that I had forgotten we were having our swimming test today. I just hoped I did not disgrace myself.

We all ran down to the lake. Sue was waiting for us. She had a whistle on a string around her neck.

"All right," she said, "stand over here if you know you are a beginner. You are the Red Caps. You must not go in over your waist until Liz teaches you how to swim." She turned to us after the Red Caps had moved over to their place. "Now for the rest of you, you may go in four at a time. Swim to the first raft. If you are tired or feel you want to stop, stay there. You will be our intermediate group, the Green Caps. If you feel fine and know you can make it out to the farther raft, go ahead. You are the Blue Caps, our top group. O.K., every-body line up here."

Sue climbed into a rowboat and nodded to the head of the line. I was standing about half-way back. The twins and two other girls went in first. I watched as they swam right out to the farthest raft. They were strong confident swimmers. I think they started taking lessons when they were about three, and they had a pool in their backyard. I could see the teacher on the raft gave each of them a blue cap, and they dove off and swam around. It looked wonderful.

Four more girls went in. I saw three of them stop at the Green Cap area, and one went on. The Red Caps were splashing around in water only up to their hips, but then Liz called them over to start teaching them to float. At least I was not a Red Cap, thank goodness. I saw Rachel go in the next group. I shaded my eyes to see how she was doing, and saw her make it out to Blue Cap. Tracy was two rows ahead of me, but then stepped out of line and came back where I was.

"I don't know about this," she said.

I saw Ursula and Heather and two more girls from their cabin go in. Heather stopped at Green Cap, but Ursula made it all the way. I wondered if being a good actress had anything to do with being a good swimmer.

Finally it was Tracy's and my turn. I felt breathless as I stepped into the lake. It was a hot day and the coolness of the water felt good, but the bottom was awful. Mud oozed up between my toes, covering half-way up my foot. Ugh! I flung my body forward into the water even though it was shallow here. I'd rather swim in three feet of water than walk through that goo. Tracy copied me, clenching her teeth. Now I was swimming, but I still felt nervous. My breath was gaspy, and I swallowed some water. Even the first raft looked pretty far out to me, but I had to make it to that. I was kicking too wildly, I knew, and spraying water around. Sue was rowing along beside us. She was looking at me thoughtfully. Tracy was gasping too. She was no better a swimmer than I was. We finally reached the raft. My arms were so tired I could hardly climb the ladder. I knew there was no point in my trying to go farther. Tracy felt the same way. The teacher on the raft smiled as we stood up shakily. She handed each of us a green cap.

"Fine," she said. "I'm Lou. You'll both be doing better in a little while. We have swimming every day."

Tracy and I sat down on the side for a few minutes to rest. The twins and Rachel looked over at us and waved. They seemed to be having a wonderful time.

"Well, you can't win 'em all," Tracy said.

I looked at a water bug floating on the surface of the water. "The trouble is," I said, "I get nervous, and that makes me breathless."

"I know. Me too."

I heard laughing voices coming from the Blue Caps. "But, so help me, I'm going to make it out there before I leave this camp!"

"Um," Tracy said. "I don't know. Does it matter?"

I nodded. "It does to me." I took her hand. "And you know what, you're coming with me." I decided right then that I was

23

going to stop being nervous about swimming and I was going to let Lou help me. If Rachel could do it, so could Tracy and I.

That evening after supper was boating time for our group. It was cooler now and we all had on jeans and sweaters. Sue met us. She told us three people could go in each rowboat. She showed us how to row: pulling the oars together to make the boat go straight, pulling on one oar while holding the other straight out to make the boat turn, pulling on one oar and pushing on the other to make the boat go in a circle. The twins and I ran for the same boat, as we struggled into our orange life-jackets. Joy told me to row.

"Turn left," Joy giggled. I did.

"Go round in a circle," Janie added. I did. But going back to the dock I got mixed up and bumped into another boat. We all laughed but the girls in the other boat looked kind of mad.

We had a special treat at the all-camp Campfire that night. One of the counselors in the Desert Area was a Native American. She had put on a beautiful leather dress with a beaded belt, and she showed us some of the real Indian dances. Her brother was visiting, and he sat on the ground and beat the tom-tom. It was wonderful. The girl bent and moved to the beat, and the fire threw light and shadows over her. The drum made us want to get up and dance too.

We all agreed that this was the best campfire program so far. We tried to do her steps going back to the cabin, but we just looked funny. We laughed all the way to the bath house. I was standing beside the basin washing my face when Ursula came in. She came to the basin beside me, but she did not look at me. I decided to try and be friendly.

"That was a wonderful program, wasn't it?" I said.

Ursula nodded, but she did not smile. "Yes."

I tried again. "You're doing a really fantastic job of the witch."

She shrugged. "Thanks."

I dried my face, thinking that she was just impossible. Well, I had tried. We all went back to our cabin and got into our sleeping bags.

Taps sounded through the camp. I looked out into the blackness of the woods. I could see a few blinking fireflies. As I looked at them my eyes became heavy. I was just going to sleep when suddenly a scream filled the cabin.

My eyes flew open. Several flashlights turned on. Joy was standing beside her bed. She was smacking at her pajamas, and shouting.

Janie jumped over beside her. "What's the matter?"

"Look at the bed," Joy pointed. "Look at me. Oh, help!"

We all looked. Big black ants were over everything; the pillow, the sleeping bag, and Joy! We all reached out and knocked them off of her. Janie grabbed the sleeping bag and shook it upside down, stepping on the ants as they fell on the floor.

"Why me?" Joy moaned. "Why did they pick me?"

Janie looked up. "Oh, I think I know." She leaned over and pulled Joy's bag from under the bed. Ants were crawling over and around it. Janie opened it and took out the box of cookies. It was full of ants. It looked horrible! Joy grabbed the box and threw it on the ground outside of the cabin. We took the insect spray can and doused her bed with it, and the floor under her bed, and the duffel. Then we sprayed her.

When we all calmed down, we went back to bed, but it was a long time before I could sleep. I felt wiggly and itchy all over. The last thing I remember was Janie saying, "I was

25

supposed to have the cookie box tomorrow. I guess I would have gotten the ants too."

And Joy answered her, "That's just what I was thinking, sister. Um!"

FOUR

The first thing the next morning we took the box of ruined cookies and put it in the trash can by the bath house. We told Terry about the ants.

She laughed and said, "Don't ever keep food in these cabins, girls. You're lucky it was just ants!" She hugged Joy with one arm and Janie with the other. "If I had realized that it was food in your surprise package I would have told you before."

She was right about bugs being in the cabin. Every day we saw more Daddy-Long-Legs. I got used to them and did not scream anymore. But a couple of days later when I woke up, I could not open my right eye. It was swollen completely shut. The girls looked at me in horror.

"What happened?" Rachel asked.

"I don't know." I felt a little frightened.

Tracy went and found Lucy. When she saw me she told me to go and see Beth, the camp nurse.

"Even if you are late to breakfast, it won't matter," Lucy said. "I'll tell Scotty you're with Beth."

She told Tracy to go with me. We went along the back path to the Infirmary cabin. Beth and Neil had a room on the back of it. Neil was coming out just as we came up.

"Hi," he said with a smile.

He was so handsome. I turned my head away and covered my eye with my hand. I knew how awful I looked. I had seen myself in the mirror.

He turned to the door and called Beth, "You've got a patient, Honey."

Beth took me right in and told me to sit on a stool beside a bright lamp. She turned the light toward my face.

"It looks terrible, doesn't it?" I said.

She smiled. Beth had a beautiful smile. "I'm sure it feels terrible, Libby, but actually by tomorrow it will be much better. A spider bit your eyelid."

A spider! How horrible! I imagined a spider crawling over me while I was sleeping, and then biting me. I shivered.

"Be sure to put on insect repellent before you go to bed," Beth added. She poured something on a cotton ball and bathed my eye with it. "It will bother you today, but in the morning it really will be better. You'll see." She handed me some ice in a paper towel.

I heard the bugle for breakfast and I stood up. "Thanks."

Neil came into the room. "O.K?" he asked me.

I turned my face away. "Yes. Just a spider bite."

He grinned. "They know a good thing when they see it!" I did not laugh and he added in a kind voice, "Does it hurt much?"

"It feels stiff . . . and big."

"It doesn't look so bad."

Tracy touched my arm. "Breakfast," she whispered.

We almost ran up the hill because we knew we were late already. I felt so stupid walking in with this fat eye. As we sat down, I whispered to Tracy, "Boy, if the queen asked the magic mirror on the wall, who was the fairest one of all, he certainly wouldn't pick me today!"

By Drama Group time, the swelling was down a little, probably because of the ice I had been using. It was a good thing I had all my lines learned. It would have been hard to try and read them with just one eye and still watch the stage.

Just before I left the cabin, Rachel handed me her sun glasses. "Wear these. It won't show as much."

The glasses did make the eye feel better, but when I came in Ursula looked over and gave me a scornful smile. I think she thought I was putting on some movie-star act, or something.

I said loudly to Claire, "Sorry about the sun glasses but a spider bit my eye last night. The light kind of hurts it."

"Oh, I'm sorry," Claire said.

I glanced at Ursula. She was still looking at me but the nasty smile was gone. I thought, I'll never understand this girl.

The rehearsal went well. We were still working on movements and where we should be on the stage.

"I was going to teach you to faint today," Claire said. "There's a right way to fall without hurting yourself. Would you rather wait because of your eye?"

"No, I can do it now." I knew I was not that much of a sissy. I saw Ursula glance curiously at me again.

"All right," Claire said, "after you take the bite of the apple, gasp a little, like this. Sway, and then just let your knees fold up under you." She showed me. "You kind of sit in slow motion, but it looks like you fell."

I tried it a few times until I could do it well. It was kind of fun.

Claire turned to Ursula. "Now, as she falls, stand for a moment and look down at her. Look triumphant and nasty. You think you have gotten rid of her. Good, that's right."

I opened my good eye and looked at Ursula. The expression on her face made me feel cold. What an amazing actress she was!

29

After the rehearsal I went back to the Infirmary to ask Beth to put some more of that medicine on my eye, and to give me some more ice. Beth said it looked better. It felt better too, but I put the sunglasses back on anyway. Neil met me at the door.

"Lady in disguise," he said. I grinned. "I hear you are acting Snow White."

"Yes."

"That's great. I'm eager to see it."

"We give the play the last day."

He nodded. "I think I'm supposed to help with the scenery."

"That's nice!" I smiled at him, and then ran down the path to our cabin to get ready for swimming. Tracy was there. The other girls had already left. I was late because I had gone to the Infirmary.

As I put on my suit, I said to Tracy, "I'm glad that test is over."

"So am I. Libby, do you think we can just swim on out to the Blue Cap whenever we want to, or do we have to wait for Lou to give us the O.K.?"

I grabbed my green cap and we banged the screen door behind us. "I think we can go when we think we're ready, but we'd better tell Lou first. She feels responsible for us." As we jumped into the water, I added, "However, one of these days I may just take off."

"Without even telling me?"

"Oh, I have to tell you. You're my buddy." As we reached the raft I said, "Tracy, don't you think Neil is kind of cute?"

"Who's Neil?"

"The handyman, Silly. Beth's husband."

"Oh, yeah. He's all right, I guess." She grinned at me. "Since you asked, I take it you like him."

"Yes, he's very nice."

We stopped talking then because it takes all my concentration to swim without gasping. I was trying very hard to keep my legs from kicking so wildly. When I reached the raft Lou was teaching some of the Green Caps the side-stroke. I listened and practiced slowly.

"Hi," someone said beside me.

It was Heather, the girl who was in Ursula's cabin.

"Oh, Hi," I said. I tried to tread water as we talked. It was six feet deep here which made me a little nervous.

"I heard that you're playing Snow White. That's great."

"It's fun."

Heather wiped water out of her eyes. "How's Ursula doing?"

"She's really good," I said. "She's a talented actress."

"Oh? She never talks about it."

I was treading water very well, so I kept doing it. "Have you known her very long, Heather?"

"No, I only met her when we came to camp. She's really hard to know. The other girls in the cabin are fine."

"I wonder what's the matter with her."

"I don't know. She's upset about something."

Lou looked over at us. "Do you want to practice your strokes, girls?"

I grinned at Heather and swam away.

"Libby," Lou called, "keep you knees straight. You're kicking up too much water."

Tracy swam up to me and then lay back in the water. "Watch me float. Not a care in the world!"

I poked her. "Lucky you!"

A wave splashed over her face and she gasped.

"Oh, you want to play rough?" She slapped the surface

of the water, and it hit me in the face. I went under for a moment and then came up laughing.

"Hey, you two," Lou called, "behave yourselves. No rough-housing."

"Yeah," I said to Tracy. "Behave yourself, and stop getting me into trouble."

"Me? Get you into trouble?" She grinned and started to swim away. "You make your own trouble, Partner—spiders, Ursula, Neil. I'm not responsible!"

As I swam in the opposite direction, I decided Tracy was right. I had a way of getting involved in things that complicated my life. My mom says I'm too curious; about people, and situations, and what's going to happen. Maybe she's right.

But now I had to concentrate on my swimming. Keep my knees straight. Close my fingers. Don't be afraid to get my face in the water. I swam around the raft four times before stopping to rest. Lou smiled approvingly at me.

After we were all in bed that night, it began to rain. It started softly, just a pattering on the roof.

"Oh, this is cozy," Rachel said.

I snuggled down into my sleeping bag, agreeing with her. But then the rain really began and the wind came in gusts. I looked nervously at the canvas roof. It was rising and falling in the wind.

"Who's afraid of the big bad wind?" Tracy sang.

We all laughed, but I knew we were nervous. A flash of lightening lit up the sky and a moment later the thunder boomed. I remember being very scared of lightening and thunder when I was little. I don't like it too much even now. Another flash came.

"I just hope", Janie mumbled, "that it doesn't hit one of those trees."

"Cheerful sister!" Joy said.

Then such a loud clap of thunder came that it shook the floor. The wind was lashing at the trees behind our cabin. Every time the lightening flashed I could see them swaying and tossing. I wondered if their roots went deep enough to keep them upright.

"Don't worry," Rachel said. "It can't keep up like this very long." She must have read my mind.

We all lay tensely, with our eyes wide open. For the first time I wished there was an adult in the cabin with us. How could the rain keep falling this heavily? I remembered summer storms when I was in my bed at home. They had not really frightened me at this age. But now I felt I was out in it, with only this flapping roof to protect me.

"Oh, no," Tracy suddenly said loudly, "I have to go to the bathroom. I don't suppose one of you wants to come with me?"

We all kind of laughed, but no one answered. After a while the storm passed, and I went to sleep. I don't know when, or if, Tracy went to the bathhouse. I wonder if anyone went with her.

FIVE

A couple of days later, during Free Time, Terry rapped on our door and said, "Tracy, someone's here to see you."

It was a hot day, and all of us were lying on our beds. Tracy even had a cold wet washcloth on her forehead, and every now and then she moaned. She likes to act dramatic even though she does not like acting in plays. Now she took the cloth off her face and sat up.

"Hi, Tracy," a man said.

We had never seen Tracy's father, but we were sure that was who it was. He had the same reddish hair and he was sort of plump. Tracy ran to the door.

"Dad!" She sounded excited and a little nervous.

He gave her a crinkly smile. "Can I come in?"

"Sure, sure." Tracy pushed open the screen door. "Gosh, I never expected to see you here."

"I had a meeting in Arborville, but I knew the camp was close. I thought I'd drop by and see how you are."

I remembered that he was divorced from her mom, and that he was a car salesman in Chicago. Also I knew that Tracy usually spent six weeks of the summer with him, but this year she would go after camp.

"I'm fine, just great," Tracy said. "These are my friends, Dad. Janie, Joy, Rachel, and Libby. We're all in school together. We're having Free Time right now, but if you can stay awhile you can see me swim." She caught my eye. "Not that I'm a great swimmer."

"Yet!" I said.

Mr. Green smiled at me. "I'm glad to meet all of you. Tracy has talked about you a lot." He looked around the cabin. "So this is where you live."

"Yeah," Tracy said, "with the spiders, mosquitoes, and ants."

"No snakes?"

Janie shuddered. "Not so far, fortunately."

"Oh, I don't know," Joy added. "That might be kind of interesting."

"For the snake, perhaps," Rachel said. "I think we could do without it."

Mr. Green nodded. "It looks as though you have gone back to nature here. Thoreau would approve of you."

I remembered hearing something about Thoreau in my English class. He lived in a little cottage beside Walden Pond, and enjoyed getting away from civilization. Thinking of the Daddy-Long-Legs, I didn't think civilization was all that bad.

"How long can you stay, Dad?" Tracy asked.

He looked at his watch. "About half an hour."

"O.K. That will give us time to show you around." She looked at us. "Come on, let's show him our camp."

Tracy and her dad started down the path. Rachel and I fell into step behind them, and the twins brought up the rear. They were still talking about what we would do if a snake showed up. I decided not to worry about it until it happened.

We walked to the lake, and the Crafts building, and then to Hilltop House. Mr. Green was really impressed with the view from up there. On the way down the hill we met Ursula coming up. As she met us she stopped and stared at Mr. Green. Tracy does not usually like Ursula, but with her staring like that she had to say something.

"This is my dad, David Green, Ursula. Dad, this is Ursula. She's in the play with Libby."

Mr. Green smiled and held out his hand, but Ursula just continued to stare and she looked upset.

"Hi," she said finally, and then she turned and ran up the hill.

Tracy shrugged. "She's weird, Dad. Don't pay any attention."

As we were walking to the Infirmary, Mr. Green took Tracy's hand. "I have something special to show you when you come to Chicago."

She grinned at him. "What is it? A dog?" Tracy really wanted a dog, and she could not have one in the apartment building where she lived with her mom. Her dad lived in a condo and dogs were allowed if they were kept on a leash. She had mentioned to us how great it would be if her dad bought a dog for her.

He seemed surprised. "Well, no. We'll think about that later." Then he paused and looked thoughtful. Rachel and I were walking behind him, but I could see his face when he turned to talk to Tracy.

"As a matter of fact, I've met someone I want you to meet."

Tracy looked alarmed. "Who?"

"Well, her name is Hazel, and she's very nice. I've been seeing a lot of her."

We knew that Tracy knew that her dad dated, but she never thought he might be serious about someone.

"As a matter of fact, she's divorced too, and she has two

boys. One is a year older than you, and one is a year younger. I thought you might like that," he said.

Tracy stopped walking and faced him. "Boys?" she repeated in disgust.

"They are very nice. I'm sure you'll think so once you get to know them. They'll be . . . almost like brothers."

Tracy frowned. "I don't want any brothers. I only want you, and mom, and me."

He shook his head. I thought he looked exasperated. "But, Honey, you know that's not the way it is anymore. You belong to both your mom and me, but we don't belong to each other. She is completely free to marry again if she wants to."

"Well, she doesn't want to." Tracy sounded belligerent.

Her dad looked thoughtful and then spoke firmly. "Now listen, Tracy. I love Hazel, and I love her boys too. She needs a husband and I need a wife. But that will not change anything between you and me. As a matter of fact, I'll be a happier man because I won't be lonely anymore. Don't you want me to be happy?"

She looked down at the ground. "I guess so."

I felt uncomfortable to be hearing this. I looked at Rachel and shrugged a bit. Joy and Janie were talking about Ursula and trying to figure out what was wrong with her. I don't think they had heard much of the conversation between Tracy and her dad.

He patted her shoulder. "Come on, Honey. Don't fight me about this. I love you. No one can take your place, ever. You know that, don't you?"

"I guess so," she said again.

"Good. And when you come to see me, we'll have a special day with the boys. We'll go to the Field Museum, and the

Planetarium, and the Aquarium, and we'll eat out. You'd like that, wouldn't you?"

"Yeah. Sure." Her tone was still sad.

He took her hand and started down the hill again. "It will take time, I know, but after you get to know them all you'll like the idea. I'm sure you will."

"Will the boys live with you?" Tracy asked.

"Most of the time, but of course they will go to their own father sometimes."

"It sounds kind of mixed up."

"I know it does now, but we'll sort it out. By the way, their names are Bruce and Tony. Bruce is the older one. They seem curious about having a red-haired sister."

Tracy suddenly looked at him. "Will they call you Dad?" she asked.

He shook his head. "No, only you will call me that. They have a father. They call me Dave." His voice sounded warm.

Tracy smiled a little. "I'm glad."

He grinned at her. "So am I!"

After that we showed him the Infirmary, and he met Beth and Neil, and then we all walked with him to the car.

"This was fun," he said. "Now I can imagine where you are." He looked at the rest of us. "It's good to meet all of you. Keep my kid out of mischief, will you?"

I nodded. "We'll try, but that's no easy job." Tracy pretended to hit me.

Her dad gave her a tight hug. "So long, Kiddo. I'll see you soon."

"Yeah. 'Bye Dad. I'm glad you came."

We all watched as he backed the car out and drove down the road.

"Boy," Tracy said, "a step-mother! That's all I need." She did not really sound too upset, and I was not worried about her now. What really stuck in my mind was the way her dad had hugged her. I remembered what it was like to have a bear-hug from a dad. It occurred to me that it was better to have a father you had to share with other people than to have him gone completely. But at least I could remember mine. In a way, I decided, I could never completely lose him as long as I remembered. I know my mom remembers too.

Janie poked my arm. "Come on, stop dreaming. We're late for swimming already." Everyone started to run.

"Last one there is a fig cookie," Joy shouted.

Of course I was the last one.

"Fig cookie," they all laughed at me.

"Fig cookies aren't so bad," I said. "It could be worse!" We banged the door behind us as we ran to the lake.

That night I woke up suddenly. I could see in the dim light that Rachel was sitting up in bed.

"What was that?" I whispered.

"I think I heard something."

"I know. I heard it too." Our conversation woke up the others.

"For goodness sake, can't a person get any sleep around here?" Tracy said crossly.

"What's the matter" Janie asked, not bothering to whisper.

"We heard something," Rachel said.

"Like what?" Joy yawned.

I took a big breath. "It sounds like a huge animal." We all listened. It was unmistakable, the sound of feet moving through the leaves, crunching the sticks.

"There is something out there," Tracy gasped, forgetting to sound cross.

"Should I shine my flashlight on it?" Janie asked uncertainly.

"Maybe not," Rachel said. "Then it will know we are in here."

"I think it knows anyway," Joy said. "Animals have a strong sense of smell. I'm sure it can smell us."

"Yeah, probably," Janie added nervously.

I was nervous too. Ordinarily I would have said something about all of us needing a bath if our smell even went outside the cabin, but I was too scared to joke. The crunching continued. It sounded close to my end.

"What kind of an animal do you think it is?" I whispered.

"Well," Rachel said, "those sounds are too big for a squirrel, or raccoon, or something like a woodchuck. It's got to be bigger than that."

"Like a bear?" Tracy asked in an awed voice.

"That's what I was thinking too," I mumbled.

"If we all scream together," Janie said, "do you think Terry would hear us?"

"Sure," Joy answered. "That would probably annoy the bear too."

"Gosh," I said, "do you think the bear will try to get in here?"

Even Joy was sounding scared now. "Well, I think his claws could tear that screen easily."

"Why would he do that?" Janie gasped.

"If he's hungry and he thinks we have food, or that we are going to try to hurt him, I guess," Joy replied.

"What can we do?" Tracy wailed.

We were all scared now. I thought I could hear breathing just outside of my window, and every now and then a twig snapped. I was even too frightened to look into the darkness closely. I was afraid I might see two glinting eyes staring at me. I wished that I could run over and get in bed with one of the other girls, but I was too shaky to move. I almost stopped breathing!

Suddenly I heard someone's feet on the floor. A body came up close to my bed, and a flashlight shone into the darkness in a solid white beam. We all looked wildly outside, terrified of what we might see. The light shone on a large head, and two startled eyes. For a moment the animal stood frozen and then bounded away, it's small antlers catching in the leaves overhead as it leaped.

"A deer," Janie said limply. She turned the flashlight into the cabin.

"How did you dare get up?" I gasped weakly. "I couldn't move."

"Sis, I'm proud of you," Joy said, "I didn't know you were so brave."

Janie shook her head. "I'm not brave. I thought it was a bear, but I had to know for sure. The suspense was worse than knowing."

"A deer," Tracy grumbled. "Just a plain old deer."

"Not plain," Rachel chuckled. "He's getting antlers."

Now that the danger was past, I was feeling brave too. "Of course there are probably many more deer in these woods than bears. I didn't think of that, but I knew it was something big."

Janie walked back to bed and turned off her flashlight. I shut my eyes and tried to get back to sleep, but I felt wide awake. I opened my eyes and stared into the darkness.

"Anybody awake?" Tracy whispered.

We all said "Yes." None of us could sleep.

"It's too bad we don't have some yummy thing to eat," Rachel said. "We could have a midnight feast."

Since the night of the ants we had not brought any food into our cabin.

"Well, we don't," I answered.

"Want to sit on the floor and play a game?" Janie asked.

"No," Joy said, "it's too cold."

We could hear her snuggling down into her sleeping bag.

"O.K.," Tracy suggested. "Ghost stories."

"Ghost stories?" I shrieked. "After we've all been scared to death?"

"Sure. What better time," Tracy laughed. "I'll give you something to really be scared about." She cleared her throat, and then spoke in an erie hollow tone. "One night in a cabin in the woods five girls were sleeping. It was a very dark night, with almost no moonlight. Suddenly they woke up. There was something outside the cabin."

I chuckled. "I think I know this story."

"Just wait," Tracy said. "It's not a deer this time." She went on talking of an enchanted prince, who was turned into a bear. She had a princess in the story named Tracy, and four servant girls named Libby, Janie, Joy, and Rachel. The story was not very scary, in fact it made me feel relaxed and calm again. About the time that the bear-prince was trying to save the princess from an evil toad, I went to sleep. The next morning I wanted to ask Tracy what had happened, but I hated to tell her I had not stayed awake. So I asked Rachel.

"I don't know," she said. "I fell asleep."

Now that was too bad, I thought. I would never know what happened to the bear-prince, and princess, and wicked toad, unless I got up nerve enough to tell Tracy her scary story had actually put me to sleep!

43

At the beginning of the second week, Terry announced at the campfire that the next day we were going to have an overnight hike. She said it would be sort of like a wilderness experience, that we would have to cook outside and use some of the materials that were available.

Tracy groaned. "Here's where I starve."

Rachel grinned. "Just don't eat toadstools"

"You will each need to take your sleeping bag, pillow, flashlight, towel, washcloth, soap, toothbrush and tooth-paste," Terry continued.

"And a comb," I muttered, "unless we want to look like cavewomen."

We were all excited about it. The next day dragged because we could hardly wait for the time to come. All of the Mountain Group was going to go, and we had been excused from swimming so we could leave at four o'clock. Ursula would be going too of course, but I was too excited to care. Terry had told us that it was not a true Wilderness Experience because we were taking food with us, but we would cook as much as possible over the campfire. In a true Wilderness Experience you eat only things you find outside. I guess that means catching fish, picking berries and mush-rooms, and leaves and greens that can be eaten. I under-stood that we were taking hot dogs and buns, and pancake mix. That sounded like a good idea to me. Somehow leaves and berries are hard to get excited about!

At four o'clock we all met at the campfire pit. I had tied up my sleeping bag and all the other things. I hoisted it up on my back, feeling like a mountain climber. The other girls did the same.

Janie said with a laugh, "All we need is a flower over each ear and we could pass as a loaded donkey."

"Yeah, a real beast of burden," Joy added.

"Well, anyway a beast!" I said.

As we were lining up Robin came over to us. "By the way, girls, we are taking four matches for each cabin, two for supper and two for breakfast. If you can't make your fire light with that number, it's back to rubbing sticks together."

"Oh, great," Tracy said. "I should have brought a magnifying glass."

"I tried that once," Rachel answered. "I held it in the sun right over a sheet of paper. I did make the paper smoke and turn brown, but I couldn't start a flame."

"I'm sure a little smoke could not cook a hot dog," Tracy said, shaking her head. "I have a feeling I really may starve in the next twenty-four hours."

"Or lose ten pounds," I grinned.

Tracy grinned back. "A fate worse than death!"

We all lined up by cabins. Terry was in the lead. She had a machete for cutting bushes to make a path. Good heavens, where were they taking us? Robin was in the middle of the line, and Lucy was at the end.

"Do they think we're going to run away and get lost?" Joy whispered.

"Like Babes in the Woods," Janie grinned. "Only we don't have any bread or stones to drop and mark the way."

Rachel took her compass out of her pocket. "At least we know the direction we're going."

"Smart girl," I said. "You're the brain around here for sure."

We all started walking. Terry headed for the woods beyond our camp. Every now and then we saw her hack at a bush across the path.

"I always wanted to go through the jungle on safari," Tracy said, "but not very much."

I smiled over my shoulder at her. I felt just a little breathless. The sleeping bag was not particularly heavy, but it was bulky. It felt as though a huge soft animal was clinging to my back. It made me glad that I did not usually walk around carrying a load like this. We went through the woods for about half an hour, passing a muddy little pond, and finally came out on a open place at the top of a hill. The trees were still around the edge, but where we were standing was flat level ground. At least it seemed to be.

"This is camp," Terry called.

"Camp?" Tracy repeated. "It looks like the back of the beyond to me!"

Rachel dropped her sleeping bag. "Well, at least it's open. I was afraid we might have to sleep in the woods back there."

Janie shook her head. "With all the leaves, moss, dirt, and roots can you imagine what creepy things are there? Ugh!"

"Still," Joy said thoughtfully, "it might be interesting."

"Yeah, if you're another bug," I answered.

Robin and Lucy came over to us and told us to pile up our sleeping bags and come sit in front of Terry. As we walked over I saw a little stream on the other side of the hill. It was bubbling over some rocks, and shining in the sun. We all sat on the ground in our jeans. Lucy had told us not to wear shorts because there were prickly bushes in the woods. She was right. I pulled a few burrs off my legs, and rubbed my shoe on the grass to wipe off some of the damp moss. It felt good to sit after that walk. I was excited to hear what we would do next.

"All right," Terry said loudly. "Now before we think about supper, we have to set up our camp. I'm going to give each cabin a job. We have to bring some water up from the stream, not to drink, but to use for washing. We need to clear some places for campfires. Some of you will cut and peel sticks for roasting the hot dogs, and some need to collect firewood. And one group will need to dig a latrine back behind those trees."

"A what?" Rachel whispered.

"Latrine," I said. "Toilet." I remembered reading in a book about Scouts doing that.

"Good heavens," Tracy grumbled, "we have to build a toilet?"

I grinned. "Just a hole in the ground with two planks to stand on."

Tracy moaned. "Civilization where are you?"

"Oh, well," Joy grinned, "this is primitive living."

"I agree with Tracy," Janie said. "It's primitive all right, but I'm not sure it's living!"

Our cabin was given the job of bringing up water from the stream. Ursula's was to dig the hole for the latrine. She looked so disgusted I thought she might refuse to do it, but Lucy was standing right there looking at her. I guess she didn't dare.

I heard Lucy say, "We'll leave one of the shovels here so each girl can put in some dirt after she uses it." I decided this *was* fairly primitive, but if you are living next to nature, that's what you get.

The five of us went down to the stream. We were each carrying two buckets. It was really pretty here. We stepped out onto some of the flat rocks in the water, and crossed to the other side. This sure beat digging holes in the ground! But going back up, we realized the buckets were heavy. It was a struggle getting them up the hill. Finally we each put one bucket on the grass, and carried just one to where Terry was. Then we ran back for the other ones. Some of the groups were still working, so we sat on the grass and looked at the clouds. We could see some that looked like animals, a poodle and a bent-up dinosaur. Then Robin came up and handed me two matches.

"Don't waste them," she said. "That's all you get. I'm keeping your other two for breakfast."

Terry and the girls from another cabin were unpacking some boxes which Neil had dropped off for us from the camp truck. He had taken the road around the woods, I guess, while we were going through it. Then Terry called out for one girl to come up from each cabin to get the food.

"You go," Rachel said to me. "Robin gave you the matches."

I put the matches safely in my pocket, and walked over to Terry. She handed me a bag. "There are two hot dogs for each of you, two buns, an apple, carrot sticks, and the makings of S'mores, and a bottle of fruit punch." She smiled. "If we were really living off the land you would have to eat off a leaf or your hand, but we decided to help you a bit. There are paper plates, cups, and napkins there too."

I carried the bag back to the girls, and we chose one of the cleared spots for our campfire. The grass had been stripped down to dirt, and we had been told to keep the fire in that area. We even found some stones and put them in a circle at the edge of the dirt so we would know how far the flame could safely spread. Rachel picked up a green stick for each of us, and Tracy brought over an armful of firewood. Janie and Joy tore up a small mound of paper, put twigs on top, and the larger sticks around. It looked like a tepee. I divided up the plates and food, and we each put a hot dog on our stick.

"Do two at a time," Rachel said. "We'll save time."

"Good idea." I nodded. "Let's go ahead and cook them, then when the fire dies down we can do the marshmallows for S'mores."

Now to light the fire. I took one match out of my pocket, and scratched it on the stone. The flame shot up, only to be blown out by the wind.

"Oh no," Tracy groaned. "Come on, girls. Stand around her and shield the match. I wonder if they're serious about just two for each meal?"

They all crowded around me. I bit my lip, and scratched our last match across the stone. Eight hands shot out and cupped around the flame. I slowly moved it to the paper and then to the top of the twigs. It lit feebly. I leaned over and blew carefully. The flame wavered and then shot up. All of us cheered!

We were starved. Food had never tasted so good. The hot dogs were burned and we had gotten a bit of dirt on them, but they were delicious. By the time we had each finished our second S'more, and gulped down the last of the fruit punch, we felt wonderful and very proud of ourselves. It was not until then that I noticed one of the other cabins had not been able to light their fire. They were all looking as though they were going to cry, when Terry brought a little lighter and lit it for them. So much for our "tough" counselors!

We grinned at each other and threw our paper plates and cups on the last of our fire.

"Some people are just more talented than others!" I said.

It was getting dark now. As soon as the last group had finished eating and cleaning up, Terry told us to pick places for our sleeping bags. She said we could wash from the cans of water that we had carried from the stream, but that there was bottled water to drink and use for our teeth.

We ran to get our sleeping bags. I studied the ground and picked a spot that looked level and smooth. The twins flopped their bags on either side of mine, and Rachel and Tracy took the outsides. We all unrolled the bags and put our pillow in place.

"Wow," I said, "this is great. Sleeping under the stars!"

We took our washcloths and soap and toothbrushes over to the cans, and laughed about washing in only a cupful of water. When everyone had finished, Terry called us into a ring in the middle of the camp. We sang rounds as the last pink faded from the sky, and the stars became bright. They looked huge out here, with no street lights to dim their light. Around the moon they were pale, but the rest of the sky was icy bright. We sang songs for about half an hour, and then Terry suggested we should go to bed.

"I know it's only eight o'clock," she said, "but you will wake up as soon as the sun is up. We'll sleep at this end instead."

We giggled and ran for our sleeping bags. I took off my jeans and shirt, and decided to sleep in my underwear.

"Be sure to put you clothes in the sleeping bag," Rachel said. "I heard Robin saying they will be wet from the dew in the morning, if we leave them out."

I snuggled into the bag and shoved my jeans and shirt in with me. Then I pulled up the zipper and lay back on the pillow.

The sky was spread out above me. The Big Dipper was so close it almost seemed that I could touch it. It was a little scary.

"G'night, kids," I said.

They mumbled goodnights, and everything was still. I looked up in awe! Wasn't this fantastic, sleeping in the open with the stars and moon so bright above me? I closed my eyes, but a few minutes later they flew open. What was the matter? I wondered, and shifted my position. I realized there was a hard area right under my back. I wriggled around some more, trying to get in a more comfortable position, but the ground seemed to be pushing against me. I might as well be lying on cement, and lumpy cement at that.

I looked at the other girls. They were all peacefully asleep. I was the only one awake! It was just me, and these huge stars, and the hard ground. I lay down with determination. I would sleep. I shut my eyes firmly, but they opened again in a few seconds. This is ridiculous, I thought. I stared at the moon noticing that it had moved a little across the sky. For hours I watched that moon! I think I slept in little bits, because when I looked again the moon had moved, but it was getting light when I finally fell asleep in spite of the hard ground under me. The next thing I knew, Joy was shaking me.

"Come on, Lazy Bones. It's six thirty."

"Time to cook breakfast," Janie said. "Everyone's up."

I groaned and sat up. I felt sore all over. I might as well be a hundred years old!

"How did you sleep?" I asked Rachel.

"Fine. I just woke up once."

"I didn't wake up at all," Tracy grinned. "This was even better than a bed."

I shook my head and pulled on my jeans. "Oh, sure. Nature's inner-spring mattress!"

Rachel looked concerned. "Didn't you sleep well, Libby?"

I made a face. "For about twenty minutes, sure. I can tell you from first-hand knowledge that the moon goes right across the sky at night. It's a fact."

"Why didn't you sleep?" Tracy asked.

We all began to roll up our sleeping bags. "It was the ground," I said. "I never felt anything so hard. I feel bruised this morning."

They all looked at me, and then Tracy laughed. "Girls, do you know we have a fairy-tale heroine right here with us? Meet the Princess and the Pea."

I couldn't help laughing too. "I would have settled for one mattress," I said. "I'm not asking for a whole pile like she had."

Terry called everyone to the center of the camp, and we all ran up to her. I looked around for Ursula. When I saw her I was surprised that she was looking at me too. I smiled at her and she gave me just a faint smile in return, then looked away. Well, I was getting somewhere! Even a small smile was better than she had been doing. Perhaps poisoning me every day in the play was making her feel better. She might even speak to me by the time the play was over.

"Now about breakfast," Terry called out. "We're having pancakes."

She handed each group a tin can. One end had been cut off, and a little door was cut in the side. We were to stand the can on our cooking spot and build a little fire inside of it. As the flame caught we were to push more twigs and paper through the door. She told us to put butter on the top of the can, and then pour half of a cup of batter on it. We were each to get three pancakes. The can was like a little stove. The only trouble was that it was impossible to control the heat. The outside of the pancakes were burned, while the inside was still runny. Tracy reached out to grab her's and burned her finger. Lucy had to put some medicine on it. Finally we put the pancakes on paper plates and poured maple syrup over them. They tasted great, although we knew no restaurant could serve them that way.

We also had orange juice and a slice of cheese. It was a good breakfast.

When we finished eating, Robin told us we had to clean up the camp site. We rolled up our sleeping bags, stamped out the fires and covered them with dirt, burned our paper trash, and put the rest in a bag to take back to Hilltop House. We covered up the latrine, and looked around to make sure we had not left one sign of our being there. When Terry was convinced it was all cleaned up, we picked up our sleeping bags and started back through the woods. I felt like a soldier coming home from a battle.

That night the other girls were talking and laughing softly after *Taps.* I think one of them said something to me, but I'm not sure. I fell into an immediate deep sleep, after a quick feeling of gratitude that there were no rocks under my back!

SEVEN

A couple of days later, we woke up to a grey sky and a soft constant rain.

"No swimming or boating today," Janie said, gloomily, as she looked outside.

"I suppose," Joy added, "the counselors will want us to spend the extra time writing letters home." She sighed.

"That's so dumb. Mom and Dad know we're all right."

"Yeah," Janie said. "If anything was wrong we'd phone. Counselors have no imagination!" The twins stood up and pretended to box each other, falling over in a heap on Joy's cot.

Rachel started to dress. "Maybe the idea is that they want us to learn how to write a decent letter."

Tracy shook her head. "And waste Alexander Graham Bell's invention? Stupid!"

Looking at the dripping rain, I said, "Anyway, this is going to continue all day. It's a good thing we have slickers."

But only the twins had thought to bring umbrellas. I decided to share Joy's, and Rachel stood next to Janie.

"Cowards," Tracy shouted. "I don't *care* if I get wet." She pulled up her slicker hood over her red hair, and dashed out of the cabin. We all watched her rush ahead to Hilltop House.

"Honestly," I mumbled, "some people will do anything for effect."

When we caught up with her inside the dining room, she was breathless, but her eyes were sparkling.

"Well there you are," she said to all of us. "I thought you would never get here!"

The rest of the morning went as usual. We doubled up under the umbrellas every time we went out, except Tracy. She continued to rush ahead of us, her slicker wrapped around her.

"She reminds me of Tigger in Winnie the Pooh," Rachel said. "Do you remember how he always rushed ahead when they were out walking?"

I sighed. "I wish she'd slow down. I'd be happy to take turns with her under this umbrella."

"You stay right where you are," Joy said. "I don't want any bouncy Tigger grabbing my umbrella."

"Wild is the word," Janie laughed. "I'm glad I've got a nice quiet Rachel."

After Crafts, Peggy suggested that we get a book from the library because we had Rest Time coming up, and swimming would be cancelled today. We each chose a couple of books and took them back to our cabin before lunch. I just hoped the rain would not make it too dark to read. There was no light in the cabin, and I didn't even have a flashlight.

At lunch Terry announced that we would have our campfire time in Hilltop House this evening because of the rain. "It will be Camp Meeting instead of Campfire this time," she said.

At the usual swimming time we all lay down on our beds to read our books. We could hear the girls from the next cabin telling jokes and laughing loudly.

"I thought this was Quiet Time," Tracy growled.

"Ignore them," Rachel said. "Pretend it's traffic noise."

56

"It sounds more like zoo noise to me," Tracy added, "except animals are cute."

I stood up and reached for my damp slicker. "Sorry to leave you, but I need to go to the bathhouse." Tracy waved a limp hand in my direction.

The rain dripped off the trees onto my head as I walked. I noticed how the smell of the green growing things around me was sharper because of the dampness. There was a low spreading juniper bush beside the path. It had a strong spicy smell that I liked.

When I went into the bathhouse I thought I heard someone crying. I stopped for a moment. Yes, a girl was standing at the end of the room by the window. She looked over at me, her eyes red with tears. It was Ursula! I didn't know what to say, and I felt very uncomfortable. I used the bathroom and washed my hands. Ursula had turned back toward the window. She was quiet now. I started to leave, but I realized I had to say something. I turned back.

"Is there anything I can do to help?" I asked. She was silent, and then she looked at me.

"There's nothing anyone can do." Her voice sounded hopeless. I just did not know what to say, but I remembered what my mom had done with a friend of her's who was unhappy.

"Do you want to talk about it?" I asked. Ursula hesitated for a moment.

"I'll tell you because you've been kind to me."

Kind? Had I been kind? I know I had had some pretty unfriendly thoughts about her. Perhaps she had not realized it. Anyway, seeing her so hopeless and sad I did not feel critical now. I smiled and leaned against the basin.

"O.K."

She took a big breath. "It's my folks. They're divorced and neither of them cares anything about me. They say they do, but I know they don't. When my dad left five years ago he took my little brother Billy. Dad likes boys!" She sounded very bitter. "I stayed with my mom. She says she loves me, but she's busy all the time with her job. She's an interior decorator, and she's always flying off to New York and hiring a sitter to stay with me. I'm just a bother to her! She'd be better off without me." Ursula wiped her eyes. "I think she sent me to camp just to get rid of me for three weeks."

It did sound kind of bleak. "That's tough," I said.

"Yes. And then when I saw Tracy with her dad, and he came all the way here to see her, I felt mad . . . and jealous too, I guess."

"Her dad's divorced too."

Ursula looked surprised. "He is?"

"And he's planning to get married again soon. Tracy's not too pleased about that."

"Oh," she said thoughtfully.

"And my dad's dead!" I don't know why I said that. I was not asking for sympathy, but I wanted Ursula to know none of us have a perfect life.

She shook her head. "That's too bad. I'm sorry."

I nodded. "We all have something."

"I guess so, but most kids have at least one parent who cares."

"Maybe your's care. They may just be too busy to show it."

"Do you think so?" Her voice was wistful, but the tears were gone.

"Well, your mom kept you. That shows something, doesn't it?"

"I guess so. But she's gone so much. I hardly know how to talk to her." She shook her head. "I'm probably not the kind of daughter she wanted. I'm fat and stupid."

I took a step toward her. "Ursula, you're not stupid. Do you know what? I think you are the best actress I have ever seen."

She looked surprised. "Really? You're not just saying that?"

"No, really. When you get older you could be a professional actress if you wanted to. I can hardly believe how good you are. I thought that the first time I heard you read."

It was strange. All my dislike of her was gone. I felt sorry for her and I wanted her to be all right.

"Gee, thanks!"

"I'm sure if your folks could see you in this play they'd be impressed."

Ursula sighed again. "Perhaps, but they can't come. They're both too busy."

I smiled. "Well, eventually they'll see you, when your name is up in lights."

Her eyes started to sparkle. "That would be great. Maybe even they would be proud of me then." She paused. "Thanks for listening to me, Libby. I'm sorry if I've been horrid to you."

"Forget it." I dried my hands and opened the door. We walked to our cabins together, with the rain in our faces. I called her attention to the smell of the juniper bushes, and she pointed out to me how many worms had crawled out of the soggy ground.

"Joy would love that," I said. "She likes worms, and bugs, and even snakes."

Ursula laughed. "Does Janie like them too?"

"No. She's into music. She plays the flute, and she's learning the recorder here at camp, and she's taking piano lessons at home."

"That's great. They sure look alike."

"Yeah, but they're really very different."

We had come to my cabin. I could see four faces peering out of the screen windows at us.

"This is where I get off," I said.

Ursula nodded. "See you at supper." She walked on.

Tracy jumped off her bed as I came in. "Did I see what I thought I saw? You mean the old witch is actually willing to walk with you?"

I took off my wet slicker and put it on the hook on the door. "She's actually kind of nice," I said. "She's had a hard time. Her folks are divorced." I decided not to say anymore than that.

Tracy looked curious. "Who does she live with, her mom or her dad?"

"Her mom."

"Um," Tracy mumbled. I knew she was thinking of her own situation. "Well, it's nice to know she's human after all."

I picked up my book and went on reading.

In Hilltop House, after supper, Scotty had us push all the tables back so we could play games. Instead of dividing us according to cabins, we were put with others who had the same birthday month. I was born August twenty-sixth, so I went to the August corner. Janie and Joy were born on July fourth. Tracy is in September, and Rachel is in October. The twins are thirteen now. I'll be thirteen next month, then Tracy and then Rachel. We tease Rachel because she's the baby of us all. Ursula came up to me in the August group.

"Really?" I said. "What date?"

"August first." She smiled.

"You almost didn't make it." I said.

Each group was a team, and we were going to play Charades. Ursula was the best. It was amazing how she could act out a title and we could understand it. I grinned at her and she nodded her head. She knew what I was thinking.

In the middle of the night I woke up and felt sick. I lay for a while hoping it would get better, but I felt worse. I got up and put on my bathrobe and sneakers, and leaned over Rachel. "Can I borrow your flashlight?"

She nodded sleepily. She probably thought I was going to the bathhouse, and I did not want to wake all of them up by telling them I was sick. I left the cabin and walked up the path to the Infirmary. The wet trees dripped around me, but the rain had stopped. I felt more and more as though I was going to throw up. I went around to the back of the room where Beth and Neil's apartment is, and knocked on the door. There was no answer, so I knocked again. I saw a light come on and Beth came to the door.

"I'm sorry to wake you but I feel kind of sick. I think I'm going to throw up."

She took me right into their little sitting room, and through the door to the Infirmary. She put her hands on my forehead and then pointed to the little bathroom.

"If you're going to be sick, Libby, do it in there."

Now I was feeling kind of dizzy too. I stumbled into the bathroom and leaned over the basin, and I did throw up. Fortunately that made me feel a bit better. I rinsed my mouth with water, and came out to Beth. She took my temperature and looked down my throat.

"Do you have a pain anywhere?" she asked.

"My tummy hurts."

She nodded. "I think you have a touch of stomach flu. You'll probably be over it tomorrow, or at least feel much better, but I'd like you to stay here tonight. Do you mind?"

I shook my head. She tucked me into a real bed, with real sheets and blankets, and my own little bathroom right there. And no Daddy-Long-Legs! I cuddled down with a sigh of comfort. I felt much better now, until I looked up and saw Neil standing in the door. I could tell he had just wakened up. I stared at him.

"Are you all right?" he asked. His hair was all mussed from sleeping.

I gulped. I wondered if he had heard me being sick? How dreadful! How could he even like me after that?

"I'm O.K." I mumbled.

He smiled and came over to the bed. "Good." He smoothed my hair back from my forehead and smiled at me. "I think you took too big a bite of that poisoned apple," he joked.

Beth looked at me. "Better now?"

"Yes. Thanks."

"Can I get you anything?"

I yawned. "No, I don't think so."

"Well, call me if you need anything. Sleep well, Honey."

Neil grinned at me. "Sleep well, Snow White." They held hands as they left me.

I turned over and sighed again. This was pure luxury! As I fell asleep bits of the play wandered through my dreams. Snow White was there, and the wicked witch, but when the prince came on, it was not the tall dark girl who played with me. This prince had blonde tousled hair and blue eyes. Even in my dream my heart ached when I looked at him! It was not until morning that I remembered I had kept Rachel's flashlight all night. I hoped she had not needed it. I felt well! The sun was shining and my mood was too.

EIGHT

As we were coming down the hill from breakfast a few days later, Beth ran up to me. It was a Saturday, although the days are all alike at camp.

"Libby," she called. "There's a phone call for you. You can take it in my room."

I looked at the other girls. "Gosh, I hope nothing's wrong at home." I ran after Beth and was breathless by the time I reached the phone. "Hello," I gasped.

"Hi, Libby." It was my mom. She sounded fine.

"Is Charles all right?" I still thought something must be wrong.

"He's right here. He wants to speak to you."

"Oh, O.K."

"Hi, Libby." Charles is three but he still sounds like a baby on the phone. "Are you having fun? What you doing?"

"Lots of things, Charlie. We swim every day, except when it rains. And we went on an overnight hike. And I'm making you something in Crafts."

"You are? What is it?"

"A surprise."

"Tell me now. I'll still be surprised."

"Well, it's a metal bolo of a lion's head." Actually I had not started that yet, but now I would have to today!

"A lion's head? Gosh!"

"What have you been doing, Charlie?"

"Mom's taking me to the zoo this afternoon. Then we're gonna get some hamburgers and milk shakes. Wouldn't you like that, Libby?"

"I sure would. It sounds great!"

"I miss you. When are you comin' home?

"In one more week, Charlie."

"Good. Don't forget to bring my lion bolo."

I laughed. "I won't forget."

"Here's Mom. Bye."

I could hear her taking the phone and saying something to him.

"I miss you too, Honey. Hiring baby sitters is for the birds!"

"You mean you miss my help," I laughed.

"I sure do, but I miss you too. Charlie and I are counting the days until you get home."

"I miss you too, Mom, but camp has been fun. I'm glad I came."

"Good." She sounded so warm and loving. I sure was lucky to have a mom like that.

"I phoned Mr. Davis last night and told him I could drive all of you home next Saturday. Charlie and I will be there for your play anyway. We're excited about seeing it."

"Yes, I'm glad you'll be there. I hope you like it."

"Oh, I know we'll like it. Well, Charlie is jumping up and down to be off to the zoo. Take care of yourself, Honey. Have a good week."

"You too, Mom. Thanks for phoning. I'll see you Saturday." I was glad the play was scheduled on a weekend. My mom is a nurse, and this next Saturday she was free. What a great mom she was. Poor Ursula! I wish she had a mom like mine.

The girls were waiting outside the door for me. Rachel reached for my hand. "Is everything all right?" she asked, sounding worried.

"Just fine. Mom just wanted to tell me that she will be driving us home next week. She's coming for the play anyway, so your dad won't have to bother, Rachel."

"Just one more week," Tracy moaned. "I'm just getting used to it."

"In spite of the wildlife?" Janie grinned.

"Maybe because of the wildlife," Joy added. The twins smiled at each other and we all started on a run to the cabin.

Later, at swimming, I was still thinking of what a sweetie my mom is. I was doing a slow backstroke around the raft, and looking up at the clouds. They were gorgeous, big and puffy. It made me feel good just to look at them. I turned on my side and did the sidestroke for awhile. No more Doggy Paddle for me! As I thought about it I glanced over at the Blue Caps' area. Maybe it was not as far out as I feared. I decided to test it. Without saying anything to anyone, I began to swim toward the Blue Caps. It was kind of far, but I kept going. I was not so breathless these days, but my arms were getting tired. I looked back at the Green Caps' raft. I was halfway between the two now, and swimming back would take as much energy as going on. I went on. Stroke! Stroke! I was tired but I had no choice. Blue Cap girls were looking out at me. I saw the twins and Rachel. As I came closer they all cheered. Finally I was there! I grabbed hold of the ladder and rested for a moment. After I caught my breath, I climbed up. The girls gathered around and banged me on the back. Ursula gave me a big grin.

The teacher, Gretchen, came over. "Did you tell Lou you were doing that?"

I gulped. "No. I didn't know if I was doing it or not."

She frowned. "Remember, you never leave your Buddy. That's a rule." Then she smiled. "All right, Libby. Welcome to the Blue Caps." She walked to the edge of the raft, and waved to Sue who was teaching in a rowboat nearby.

"Sue," she called, "please tell Lou that Libby is a Blue Cap now." Sue nodded and turned the boat toward the Green Cap raft.

I called out, "And Sue, please tell Tracy I'm sorry. It just happened!"

When we were back at the cabin after swimming, Tracy gave me a disgusted look. "What'd you mean, 'just happened'? Don't you know what you're doing?"

I shook my head. "No, really! I was just testing to see if I could make it. The next thing I knew, I was there."

"Fine friend you are! I thought you said you were taking me with you."

"I am," I said.

"Oh? When?"

I grinned. "Tomorrow. You'll see."

All the next morning Tracy kept saying, "I'll never make it."

"Yes, you will."

"No, I won't. I'll drown."

I hugged her. "They won't let you drown."

"They won't notice, and I'll drown swallowing all that muddy water. Then you'll be sorry!"

When we went in the lake that afternoon, I hung back and swam right beside Tracy. When we reached the Green Cap raft, she started to turn toward it. I began to tread water.

"Why don't you try it?" Tracy gave me a wild look. She glanced at her own raft and then out to the Blue Caps. "I'll stay right beside you," I said. "I know you can make it."

She flopped around for a few seconds, and then set her jaw. "Lou," she shouted, "I'm trying for Blue Cap, watch me!"

Lou waved and motioned to Sue to follow us in the boat.

Tracy started off with a kind of sloppy crawl. I stayed out of her way, but swam along-side.

"I should never have let you talk me into this," she sputtered.

"Hush," I said. "Keep swimming."

She did, arm over arm. As we got closer, she began to grin. "I'm going to make it," she gasped. "I *am* smart!"

I thought of Peter Pan crowing, "Oh, the cleverness of me!" But I didn't say anything.

Tracy climbed the ladder and collapsed on the raft. Girls crowded around her, and Gretchen waved at Lou.

"You're a Blue Cap," Rachel beamed. "Now we all are."

Tracy nodded and sat up. Gretchen came over. "Congratulations, Tracy. We're practicing our dives today. Would you like to join us?"

Tracy shaded her eyes and looked up. "If it's all right with you I'd like to just rest for the swim going back."

Gretchen nodded. I joined the other girls, even though I did not know much about diving. Gretchen explained it to me. "Libby, start by leaning over. Put your arms out. Duck your head down, and just drop into the water arms first."

I tried it. The first time I did sort of a belly-smack. Gretchen said it was because I went in too flat. "Lean over farther. Picture your fingers, then your head, then your body all going straight down."

The second time I did better. It was a wonderful feeling, like a shaft of light cutting down through the water. Then Gretchen called us all together. She divided us into two teams, and said we were going to have a relay race.

"This will give you practice swimming under water, and retrieving an object," she said. She held up two large tin cans. A rope was tied around each of them, and the other end was tied to the dock. She threw the cans into the water.

"The first two people dive in, open your eyes and get the can. Hold it up so we can see you have it, then drop it back in. Swim back to the raft and touch the hand of the next girl in line. Then she goes in. The first team to have you all get the can, wins."

I was third in line. Both the twins and Rachel were on the other team, but Ursula was right in front of me. When our first girl dove in I was so excited I began jumping up and down. She found the can right away, and climbed back on the raft and slapped Ursula's hand. Ursula dove in. I watched her through the water as she grabbed the can and came to the surface with it. Girls on both teams were screaming. Ursula dropped the can, and climbed back up.

"Good luck," she gasped, as she tapped my hand.

I didn't dare dive in. I jumped, holding my nose, because I had seen right where the can went down. As the water covered me I tried to open my eyes, but I had never done that before and my eyes started to sting. I closed them again and waved my arms around wildly. I knew in a moment I would have to go up for a breath, and I was wasting time. Then my hand hit something. It was the rope! I quickly pulled it up and the can came with it. I grabbed the can and bobbed to the surface. My team cheered. Quickly I dropped the can and swam to the raft.

Ursula smiled as I took my place back in line. "You did that fast. That's great!"

It was not actually until that moment that I realized perhaps I had done something dishonest. I had not actually seen the can. I had bumped into the rope. I looked down at the raft, not knowing how to answer.

The girls all started to scream as the last people went in. I screamed too, in spite of the guilty feeling I had. Both girls found their cans and swam back, but the one on the other team won by about five seconds.

Gretchen laughed. "The Winners," she said, holding up the hand of the first girl in line. "But it was close."

"Don't we get a prize?" one of the winning girls asked.

Gretchen nodded. "You sure do—satisfaction at a well-played game."

"I'd rather have a sucker," someone muttered.

It was time to swim back to shore. Ursula came over to me. "We get our costumes for the play tomorrow," she said. "Beth has finished them."

"Oh, that's right."

She looked at me quickly. "Is something wrong?"

I decided to tell her. "I didn't do the relay right. I never saw the can! I pulled it up by the rope."

She patted my arm. "Well, it wasn't your fault you bumped into the rope. You weren't trying to cheat. Forget about it!" It was hard to believe that this was my wicked witch!

I smiled at her, and then I went over and shoved Tracy with my foot. "Get up, Lazy Bones. Swimming is over."

She sat up. "If I drown going back will you save me?"

"No," I said, "but if you're a good girl Ursula might." Tracy and Ursula grinned at each other and we all plunged into the water together.

That night as we were returning from Campfire, Rachel stopped in the cabin door and gasped. A snake was hanging from the beam at the top of the roof. It was swaying back

69

and forth as though it was considering coming down. We all ran out of the door.

"I think," Joy said, "that is a harmless snake. I think!"

"You *think*," Janie echoed. "I'd like you to be *sure,* Sister."

"Well, there are very few poisonous snakes around here," Joy said.

"Suppose this is one of the few," Janie added.

"Shall I play my recorder for it? Perhaps I could hypnotize it."

"No," Rachel said. "Let's get help."

I agreed. I saw Neil and Beth down the path, leaving the campfire.

"Neil. Neil," I shouted. "Help!"

He looked across at us, and they both came over. "What's the matter? Is that old witch still chasing you?"

Tracy looked at him scornfully. "Look in there, Neil."

He looked, as Tracy shone her flashlight into our cabin. "Well, you have company," he said. He looked around and picked up a stick from the ground. Tracy kept her flashlight on, as he went in and lifted the snake down with the stick. It coiled and twisted as he carried it out and dropped it on a pile of leaves. We watched it slither away.

"Don't you think you should kill it?" Tracy asked.

"Oh, no. It's harmless, and it eats some things you wouldn't want in your tent." "

Don't tell me what," Tracy answered. Neil grinned.

"Thanks," I said. "We were sort of scared."

"I wasn't scared in the least!" Joy added.

After a moment, Janie added, "Well, I wasn't either . . . much! Remember I wanted to play my recorder for it."

"I think we were all a little scared," Rachel said.

I looked at Neil. "I wasn't exactly scared, but there are other things I would rather have as a room-mate."

70

"Me too," he said, winking at Beth.

After we were all in bed, we kept thinking about the snake.

"After all," Tracy said, "it got in once. How do we know it won't get in again?"

"It won't!" Joy said definitely. "We're all in here now. The snake won't take on all of us."

"Well, anyway," Janie said with a laugh, "if it comes back I'll play my recorder. That should keep it calm."

"Or make it bite you," Tracy growled. "It may not be a musical snake, you know."

"Girls! Girls!" Rachel said. "It takes more than a snake to make us argue. Anyway, if it comes back we'll all attack it together. That should take care of it."

"One for all, and all for one!" I said sleepily.

The snake did not come back, but the next few days we stopped each time before we went into the cabin and looked carefully at the top beam. None of us forgot about that snake!

At Hilltop House the next morning, Beth was waiting with our costumes. She had patterned mine from the cartoon movie of Snow White. As I put the yellow satin dress over my head and fastened on the blue cape with the stand-up collar, I really felt like a princess. Beth had made Ursula an old grey dress, covered by a long black cape. There was also a white wig with the hair hanging down in limp strands.

"That's just right," Beth said, studying her.

Ursula looked questioningly at me. "It's great," I nodded.

"You look gorgeous," she answered. "The heroine always gets the pretty costume."

"Old witches are not supposed to look pretty," I said with a grin. "Then the magic mirror might continue to pick you out as the fairest in the land, and poor Snow White would be ignored." Ursula laughed.

The girl playing the queen did look beautiful though. Her dress was similar to mine, but she wore a jeweled head-dress that covered her hair and she did not have a cape. Also her sleeves had fur around her wrists. I really thought she looked prettier than I did. The costume for the prince was just right. It was long tights and a short cape. Even the girl's short hair was right for the part. The animal costumes were adorable. Beth had used fake fur for the tails and ears, and she drew on whiskers and face marks with an eyebrow pencil. We were all impressed with her work, and we told her so.

Neil looked up from where he was putting the last green paint on a cardboard tree. He had decided to make just a little scenery for each scene. For the palace he had made a gold wall panel, to which he had fastened the magic mirror. The mirror was cut out of tagboard and covered with aluminum foil. Claire was going to be the voice of the mirror and the narrator, from her chair at the side. For the forest scene, Neil had made two trees that would stand at either side of the stage. The dwarfs' cottage was the best piece.

He had painted a cute little roof, held up by two pieces like the sides of a house. It gave a cozy feeling to the scene even though most of the stage was bare. For the last scene in the forest the two trees would be returned, and the table that was supposed to be Snow White's coffin would stand between them. We were not bothering with the glass cover to the coffin. The audience would just have to imagine that.

Our stage was the end of the dining room, by the kitchen door. We had no curtain, but Claire had suggested that two of the girls could carry on two folding screens. They would put them in front of our stage each time the scene was changed. After I fell on the floor from biting the poison apple, the girls would put the screens in place and I could walk to the coffin without the audience seeing me. Claire had thought of everything.

Now she looked at all of our costumes and beamed. "You all look great. Beth, you did a wonderful job!"

Our rehearsal was the best we had ever done. The costumes helped make us feel like the characters we were playing. You just don't feel like a story-book princess in shorts or jeans! The whole camp had been invited to come to our play, and any parents who were on the hill. It sounded as though we would have a good audience.

While Ursula was playing the witch, she was just as mean as ever, but when she was not acting she smiled and was friendly.

"With that costume," I said, "you really do look like a witch. I almost feel scared. What an actress you are!"

She grinned. "Good, I'm supposed to scare you. I even scare myself when I look in the mirror." I laughed. She shook her head sadly. "Only three more days of camp. I wish it could go on and on."

"Maybe we can all come again next year," I said. "Do you think your folks would let you?"

She shrugged. "I don't know why not. It doesn't make any difference in their lives."

Another idea occurred to me. "Maybe we could write to each other this year. Would you like that?"

Her eyes brightened. "Yes I really would. That's a great idea, Libby."

"You can tell me about what you're doing in school, and if you are in any plays. And I promise to write back."

"A pen-pal," she said. "That's a really nice idea."

The next two days we practiced with our costumes and scenery, and using the screens. The play seemed to be as good as we could make it. Friday afternoon during Free Time we all ran around with our autograph books getting everyone's address. Tracy had brought a camera, and she took pictures of all the counselors and around the camp. She asked Terry to take one picture for us. It showed all five of us standing in front of our cabin. Tracy said she would have five copies made of that one.

Our Campfire that night was special. The whole camp met together, and all of the counselors spoke for a few minutes. They said how much they would miss us and what a good group we had been. And then we sang songs. Claire took out her guitar and we sang, "The golden day is dying beyond the purple hills." It sounded so sad. A couple of girls looked as if they were going to cry, but then Neil stood up and told some jokes. I would miss Neil. It seemed as though I had known him much longer than just three weeks!

As we went to bed I was still feeling rather sad. I think the other girls were too. Camp had been such a wonderful adventure, even the Overnight and the snake. I felt closer to my four friends than I ever had before, and I had made some new friends as well. As *Taps* ended, I stared into the dark trees. They had become friends too. I felt both happy and sad as I went to sleep.

As soon as our alarm clock rang the next morning, I jumped up. I wanted to pack everything before the play. Fortunately there was not much to pack! After breakfast we were all to go to our Interest Groups right away. There were no chores or crafts today, and the play was at ten o'clock.

"It's going to seem strange saying goodbye to my music group," Janie said. "I'm going to ask my folks to buy me a recorder when I get home. I'm pretty good at it now."

Joy looked at her with a laugh. "Good idea. I think I'll ask them to buy me a snake."

Janie poked her in the arm. "Dopey!"

"Je suis tres content!" Rachel said, showing off her French. "That means I'm very happy."

Tracy grinned. "Impressive! Now in my math group I've learned that two and two make four. It took a long time but I've mastered it."

I laughed. "Well, I've learned not to eat poisoned apples." A feeling of excitement rose up in me. "You'll see what I've learned at ten o'clock."

"I can hardly wait," Rachel smiled. "Here we are rooming with a genuine actress!"

"What's an actress compared to knowing two and two make four?" Tracy retorted.

The bugle blew for breakfast and we all ran out, leaving our rolled up sleeping bags and cases on the beds. The cabin looked strange already, with everything packed.

After breakfast the girls left for the last session of their Interest Group. As soon as the dining room was cleared, we actors pulled our costumes and scenery out of the kitchen and stood up the screens for privacy. Beth and Neil pushed the tables back against the walls, and lined up the benches across the room for the audience.

"You're doing a great job," Neil said to me as he passed me. "As far as I'm concerned, you *are* Snow White."

"Thanks." I smiled at him. "Your scenery is great too, and Beth's costumes are wonderful."

"Joint effort," he said. "We all help each other." I noticed again how blue his eyes were and what a lovely crinkly smile he had. I sighed. I was sure I would never forget him, or Beth either. They were both very special.

"Break a leg, Libby," he said. I knew that meant 'good luck' to an actor.

"Right, and thanks for everything, Neil. I hope . . . I hope your classes go well in the fall. You should be a super teacher!"

"I hope so. If I could have a whole class of Libbys, I'm sure I would be."

We smiled at each other and he left to move another bench. I peeked around the folding screen. A few parents were seated already, but I did not see my mom and Charles. Even if they were there, I could not go and speak to them. I was already in costume, and I would have to wait until the play was over. There was still half an hour to go, and I was feeling more and more excited. Some of the girls brought out the palace hanging and the mirror for the first scene. Claire was in and out of the kitchen, checking on everything. I peeked around the screen again to see if my mom had arrived.

Ursula came out of the kitchen. "Not here yet?" she asked.

"No, but they will be."

Ursula looked through a slit in the screen. Suddenly she gasped. "Oh, no! No!" She was laughing and crying at the same time. I looked at her in surprise. She grabbed me. "Libby, my dad is there. I can't believe it. I wrote him about the play, but I never thought he would come." She peeked out again. "My brother Billy is with him. I can't believe it!"

"I'm so glad." I hugged her. "That's wonderful."

"Now we've got to do a really good job," she said with determination. "I've got to be *mean*." She pretended to choke me.

I grinned. "Just act, girl. You don't really have to kill me."

She laughed, but brushed her hand across her eyes.

A few minutes later I saw my mom come in, holding Charlie by the hand. I felt so happy! Now I could concentrate on doing a good job.

The play went well. It was the best we had ever done it. The audience clapped a long time, and some of the campers whistled. Claire looked over at us and smiled. We knew she was pleased. After taking a bow, we all ran out to speak to our folks. I went straight to my mom. Ursula jerked off her wig and ran to her dad.

Mom put her arms around me. "That was just wonderful."

Charles looked up at me. "Weren't you scared of that mean witch, Libby?"

Rachel, Tracy, Janie, and Joy crowded around me, clapping me on the back. "Fame! Fame!" Tracy said. "She'll never be the same."

Ursula brought her dad over to me. "Libby, this is my dad."

He was a big man, kind of gruff-looking, but shy too. "You did a good job," he said. He put an uncertain hand on Ursula's shoulder. "My girl did too." I could see he did care about her, but perhaps he didn't know how to show it. Perhaps she would believe it now. Ursula looked at him with big eyes. Billy grabbed her hand and swung it back and forth.

My mom reached out to her. "So this is Ursula. Libby wrote me about you. You're a wonderful actress. You really are." Mom gave her a hug. Ursula looked surprised and pleased.

Then everything seemed to happen at once. Beth and Neil came over to get our costumes. They both hugged me, and I realized I had kind of a lump in my throat. I saw my mom thanking Scotty and Terry, and the twins were getting Lucy and Robin's autograph. A couple of the campers were crying, but I was certainly not going to do that. Not at my age!

My mom and Charlie walked down to the cabin with us. "Notice how far out the Blue Cap raft is," I said. "I swam to that."

"Wow!" Charlie said.

Ursula stopped me at the door of our cabin. "I'm leaving now, Libby. My dad's going to drive me so I won't be taking the camp bus."

I smiled at her. "Good Luck."

"You too, and thanks."

I nodded. I was sure we would write to each other.

We all piled into the cabin. Charlie looked up. "Was that where the snake was?"

"Right there," I said, "hanging down."

"Gosh!" He took my mom's hand.

We all picked up our luggage, and mom held the door open for us. On the path to the car, girls kept shouting good-bye to us. Even I was beginning to feel a bit sniffley. Scotty was standing at the entrance cabin. She came over to tell us goodbye as we were piling our things in the back of our van. My friends climbed into the middle seats, and I looked at them gratefully. Thank goodness I was not leaving them! My mom started the car, and I waved at Scotty. As we drove under the big CAMP ADVENTURE sign, I leaned back in my seat. I would never forget this summer. I was sure of that. However, in a month school would start and we would all go into seventh grade. That would be our next adventure. Wow! I took a big breath and grinned at my pals in the back seats.